EP

5 Stories

Also by Keith Minnion

Novels
The Bone Worms
Dog Star
Ameri-Scares Pennsylvania: The Ghost Notes

Story Collections
It's For You
Down There & Others
The Boneyard
Read Me & Other Ghost Stories
Under The Wing & Others

Chapbooks
The Shadow on the Shade
Island Funeral

Art Books
Dark Work

EP

5 Stories

KEITH MINNION

White Noise Press

Staunton, Virginia
2025

*This one is for
my grandson Chase.*

*I've read his stuff
before any of you ever will
(and you will, you lucky bastards).*

ISBN: 978-0-9961121-9-2
Copyright © 2025

FIRST EDITION

Contact White Noise Press:
kminnion@gmail.com

The stories in this book are works of fiction.
Any resemblance that may seem to exist to actual persons,
alive or dead, is purely coincidental.

*(Cover: Moonscape; oil on canvas;
26x26"; by the author; 2023)*

WHITE
NOISE
PRESS

Contents

Maybe Not   7

Local Art   18

The Succubus

     Deæ Matres   23

     The Rest Is Yours   37

Behind Me   44

Addenda   48

Maybe Not

Martin felt the new phone vibrate in his pocket at the same time it made a chiming sound. "That means you just got a text," his daughter Philippa explained to him when she showed him how it worked.

"What do you mean? Like a letter?"

"Like an email." She saw his brow wrinkle. "Like a message, a phone call, but typed."

"But this is a phone. Why type it on a phone? Why not just call me?"

"It's just how people do it now, Dad."

He pulled the phone out now, saw his daughter's name flash momentarily on the screen, then saw a little '1' in a red circle appear on the green 'T' app. So instead of calling him, Philippa had texted.

Fine. Whatever.

Hey Dad! Taking Cindy to the new park. Wanna come?

He typed his reply slowly, with his forefinger: *I heard it might snow.*

We r living dangerously. Pick u up in 10?

God he hated this.

He saw a blue 'thumb's-up' cartoon at the bottom of the screen, and tapped it.

His daughter replied with a cartoon of her own: a little yellow smiling face wearing sunglasses.

He re-pocketed the phone, and glanced down at the mystery novel on the hassock, tented open at Chapter Six. The prose was as bland as drying mud, and he had already figured out who hanged the girl in the barn in Chapter One. He rose with a quiet grunt, and went to fetch his coat.

There were benches along one side of the play area. He chose one nearest to the huge, multi-colored jungle gym Cindy had made a bee-line for, gleefully screaming as she disappeared inside it. His daughter took a seat beside him.

"I'm surprised the town decided to build a playground here," he said, after a moment.

Philippa had begun rooting in her shoulder bag, emerging with a juice box. "Why's that?"

"It used to be a family graveyard."

"Seriously?" She stuck the little plastic straw in, and offered it to him.

He shook his head. "This was a farm once. They had a family graveyard on the property." He pointed. "Right about where those see-saws are now."

She looked. "Really? An actual cemetery?"

He shook his head again. "Graveyard. Cemeteries are near churches. No church around here." He pointed. "An old farmhouse there, though."

"Weird." She began drinking the juice box herself. "How do you know all this?"

"We used to play around here, when I was a little kid. Dare each other to run to the farmhouse and touch the porch, bang the front door. Stuff like that. We were convinced it was haunted."

"What did the family think about it?"

He gave a short, quiet laugh. "No family. It was empty, abandoned long before I was born. Definitely haunted, though. Like the little graveyard."

She took a long suck on the juice box. "So what happened to them? The gravestones? My God, the bodies?"

He pointed again. "Looks like they were moved over there. Near where the house used to be." Well beyond the playground was a small flat area in the wild grass of the field, roughly mowed, surrounded by a black iron fence.

"I wondered what that was." Philippa looked at it for a moment. "Are the stones still–?"

Cindy came rushing up, her cheeks bright pink. "Can we go swing now?"

"Would you like your juice box first, sweetie?"

Cindy's pig-tails flew in a dramatic 'no'. "Swing first!"

Philippa turned to him. "Looks like you're up, PopPop."

He heaved himself upright. "Swing time for Cindydoodle."

"YAY!" She took his hand and led him over to the kiddie swings. Red was her favorite color, he knew, but the two red kiddie seats were taken. They had a choice between the yellow and the green one.

"Which color?"

"Red!"

"No empty red ones, sweetpea. You can pick green or yellow."

She grinned mischievously "Blue!"

He looked down at her along his nose. "Cynthia Anne."

"Green."

"Green it is." He lifted her up and managed to get her little legs through the leg holes on the first try.

"Swing me high, PopPop."

"Absotively!" He pulled her back as far as he could. "Ready?"

Cindy only squealed.

They swung for a good minute, getting into a rhythm pleasing to them both, before he let his attention wander. The swings faced the field where the old farmhouse had been. A low stone wall topped with a metal rail fence surrounded the playground. Several young mothers sat along the flat top ledge of the lower wall, their gayly colored shoulder bags beside them, watching their children play. When he first saw the child standing just beyond the fence, looking through, he assumed she was with one of those mothers. But then he considered the sharp, arrowhead-shaped tips to the vertical bars of the top portion of the playground fence; surely it was too dangerous for anyone to climb over, and the only gate was at the far side of the playground, by the parking lot. What was she doing there, alone, beyond the fence? But that wasn't the oddest part. The oddest part was–

"Higher, PopPop! Higher!"

He startled, his granddaughter in the plastic swing seat momentarily filling his vision as Cindy swung back toward him. He reached out and gave her a powerful push. "YAY!" she shrieked.

Beyond her kicking legs, beyond the low wall ledge and metal fence, the girl standing outside the playground was gone.

"I saw her, swear to God." Martin regarded his beer before looking up. "Honest truth."

Eddie, on the barstool beside him, screwed up his face. "Where was this again?"

"That new playground they just built, off 33."

"I'm not placing it."

"The Shifflet farm. Where we used to play when we were kids." Martin took a quick swallow, and belched quietly. "You remember. The old haunted house in the field."

"They built a *playground* there?"

Martin nodded. "And I saw her."

The bar, already quiet this early in the afternoon, seemed to grow quieter.

"You're messing with me," Eddie said, finally. He took up his own beer, then put it back down. "This is a joke, right? What do you mean, *her?*"

"A girl. A ghost of a girl. She was there, for just a moment. I saw her, Eddie." Martin paused to take in a breath. "And I think she saw me."

Eddie stared at him, blank-faced. Then he laughed, but there was nothing in it but air. "Hey Stella! You hear any of this?"

The bartender came down to their end of the bar. "Hear what?"

"You ever hear about ghosts out at the old Shifflet farm?"

"I never even heard of the Shifflet farm. How old do you think I am?"

"It was haunted," Martin said, a note of protest in his voice. "We both knew it, when we were kids."

"Definitely before my time." She pointed to Martin's nearly empty glass.

He put his hand over it. "I saw a ghost yesterday, Stel. Same place where the haunted house used to be."

She nodded gravely. "The Shifflet farm."

Martin nodded back. "Yesterday morning. With my daughter Philippa and my granddaughter."

"In broad daylight? Did they see it?"

"No. I don't think so. But here's the thing. The odd part, the weird part."

Stella and Eddie looked at him.

"This little girl? She was all in black and white."

Stella pointed to her blouse. "Her clothes, you mean?"

"All of her. Dress, hair, skin, no color at all. Like she stepped out of an old black and white movie."

Eddie gestured to the glasses case in Martin's shirt pocket. "Were you wearing those?"

Martin felt his cheeks burn. "Nothing wrong with my eyes."

"Well, maybe, you know…"

Martin got up, adjusted his coat, and pointed to the ten by his glass. "Keep the change," he said, and left the bar without another word.

The next morning Martin awoke to dim light and a leaden sky outside his bedroom window, one more day threatening snow. With coffee and dry toast churning in his belly, he made his way from his apartment house to the bus stop at the corner in time to catch the 9:15. He flashed his senior card to the bus driver, and found a window seat halfway down, the one with the heater vent underneath. The vent curled warm air around his ankles. Across the aisle, a little boy stared at him with big moon eyes. "Leave the nice man alone," his mother said, nudging him with her elbow.

"He looks like Papa," the boy said. "Hey mister, are you a Papa?"

Martin hesitated, then nodded. "I am indeed."

"Hush now." The mother put her arm around the boy. "Sorry to bother you."

"No bother at all," Martin said.

He got off before them, winking at the little boy as he stood.

A cold breeze whipped down the sidewalk, carrying a spattering promise of snow. During the four blocks to the playground, the intermittent snow showers fell enough for him to wish he had worn his hat. By the time he reached the playground parking lot, however, it had stopped, leaving just a coating on the ground. He counted two cars in the lot, two mothers with two children each, braving the dismal day to have the playground to themselves.

He used his coat-sleeve to dry the bench he chose, off to the side, overlooking the jungle gym and seesaws, and sat. He listened to the children laughing, screaming, talking excitedly to one another, their mothers only calling out when necessary. Closing his eyes briefly, he remembered running across the road with his friends, Eddie among them, scattering into the tall, wild grass of the field with their handmade hanger and rubber-band slingshots jammed in their back jean pockets, sneaking up on the old farmhouse, hidden, crawling on their hands and knees like army men.

When he opened his eyes, he saw her.

She sat on one end of the farthest of the three seesaws, a blot of gray and black, sharing the plank with a little boy in a bright blue snowsuit and orange knit hat. She had no color at all, just grays and blacks, like the last time. Her skin, her face, her hands, were chalky white.

She turned her head to look at him with black, button eyes, and grinned. How many teeth did young children have? Twenty? Maybe a few more? This grin revealed twice as many as that. Thin, sharp, and long. Feral.

Their eyes locked. Her grin widened, impossibly. Wide enough to stuff the head of the child opposite her all the way in, all the way down, and bite it off.

He made a soft, mewling sound as he tried to rise, to gather enough courage to run over, knock the monster off her perch, save the child. He stumbled as he did so, however, and when he regained his feet he heard a thump and the little boy cry out. His end of the seesaw had dropped to the ground, jarring, scaring him. And the other end of the plank was empty. No little girl. No monster.

He looked around wildly as the boy's mother ran to her child.

Where had she gone?

The snow. Just a dusting, not even a quarter-inch of it, was mostly undisturbed around her end of the seesaw, except for a single, faint trail of child-sized shoe prints, in a straight line to the playground fence. He turned to the field beyond the playground. The snow on the roughly mowed grass seemed undisturbed; in the graveyard beyond, the stones were perfectly crowned in white.

With a burst of energy that surprised him, he exited the playground, rounded it, then struck out across the field, to the graveyard. The fence around it was tall, wrought iron, old-looking but solid, and painted black. Its narrow gate was locked with two loops of rusty chain. He looked through the bars, trying to decipher the names and dates on the stones. He found the one he was seeking off in a corner, small, half as high as the others. Its surface was weathered, and mottled with flaked green moss, but he could still read it, just as he had over half a century before.

Her name was Dorothy.

He remembered the final sling-shot attack on the old farmhouse, its few remaining panes of glass the elusive prize, before the bulldozer and back-hoe crews would arrive and chase them away, forever.

He was leading the charge across the field this final day, crawling in the tall grass and weeds, when old, weathered gravestones appeared before him, three in a ragged row, their tops hidden just below the tallest grass. The one closest to him had a name, an inscription, and dates still readable:

DOROTHY ELIZABETH
Surrendered To The Lord Too Soon
May 13 1852 – March 4 1860

Just a kid, just a year younger than him. Weird. Spooky, even. He used the stone to steady his arm, loaded his slingshot with a cats-eye marble, and leaned forward, putting his full weight on the stone to—

—And the stone cracked horizontally, down low, and gave way, sending him sprawling across the root of it still planted firmly in the ground, and banging his chin on the broken top piece, drawing blood, and a curse word he had only heard his father utter when he thought no one would hear.

He rubbed the gray stubble on his chin, remembering the pain from so long ago. Whoever had moved the graves had discarded the bottom piece of this one, and just planted the top piece over Dorothy's new grave. Sixty-two years. Remembering the coppery taste of blood in his mouth, so sure he had loosened a tooth, both angry and embarrassed at the broken stone, and having missed his shot…

"You little bitch," he breathed, his words clouding the air. "You poor little bitch."

He returned to the playground, saw the little boy in the blue snowsuit laughing as his mother pushed him on the swings, and turned to make his way through the crunching snow, back the four blocks to the bus stop. Nothing had been resolved, but he swore to himself: Cindy would never play there again, never ever. Not if he had anything to say about it.

Behind him, as he stayed to the sidewalks, little shoe prints followed.

He awoke with a start, feeling a heaviness on him, weighing him down. Outside, a night wind blew snow against his bedroom window. Across the room, the mirror over his dresser caught the bathroom nightlight spilling into the hall.

As he moved to roll over, he caught a flash of movement there, a vague shadow dashing down the hall—

He flung the covers off and staggered upright, gasping, the cold in the room joining a shock of frigid, shivering fear.

The soft machine-gun pattering of snow against the window glass was the only sound in the room. Beyond his open bedroom door, down the short hall, only darkness lay past the bathroom. The baseball bat he kept beside the nightstand seemed totally inadequate, but he took it up anyway. He stopped at the doorway. No one could be out there, he was certain. He distinctly remembered locking the apartment door when he returned home, and throwing the deadbolt before bed. All three of the windows in his apartment were closed and locked.

This is ridiculous. He looked down at the bat. *Really?*

His apartment was small, so it only took moments to search it, including the closets. The front door, the windows, all still locked, everything secure. No one was there. He returned to his bedroom, breathing heavily, and tossed the bat onto his bed. Then he willed himself to look into the dresser mirror.

She stood in the hallway, reflected there, a solid silhouette against the bathroom's night light, at a spot he had just walked through, seconds before.

He reached the bedroom door in a single leap to slam it shut, and turn the knob lock.

I'm dreaming. It's a nightmare, that's all. She can't be here, can she…?

He stepped back. As he did so, a cobweb brushed the back of his neck.

He swatted at it with a cry, then grabbed clumsily for the bat on the bed, and raised it with both hands. "Where are you?"

A creak. He turned, swinging the bat clumsily before him.

"Dammit! Stop hiding!"

"I know you."

The child's voice was hollow, full of air, just above a whisper. Dear God! *How to answer that? What to say?*

"You can't know me," he replied, finally. "I was only there twice."

"No. I saw you lots of times."

"That's not true!"

"I saw you lots of times. Being naughty."

He blinked in the darkness. "I don't understand."

"You broke Papa's windows. I saw you. I saw all of you."

He felt his throat drying up. "But that– That was–"

"And you broke my stone."

He opened his mouth, but nothing came out.

"I will never forgive you for that," she said. "Never, ever."

"Is– Is that why you're here? To scare me? To haunt me? Even here?"

Her abrupt laughter was like tiny glass bells, shattering all at once.

That angered him enough to take a step forward. "Why do you haunt the children in the playground, then? Why scare them? They never did anything to you."

A pause, then, "Because."

"Because why?"

"Because I want to play."

He sputtered, now. "What did you say?"

He heard the glass-shattered trill of laughter again, from somewhere behind him. He wheeled around, searching into the shadows, but she wasn't there. She wasn't anywhere. Only in his ears, in his head.

"They play with me," she said.

He thought of his granddaughter, playing with...this, this *thing*. "No," he said. "You have to stop. You have to go, wherever that is. You have to go!"

"Maybe." Her tone was thoughtful. "But first–"

The glass of his bedroom's only window exploded into the room; the curtains were sucked out momentarily, then blew back in, a strong gust of wind sending a flurry of snow into the room. The dozens of glass shards that struck his exposed skin made him shriek as he staggered back, dropping the bat. Both the pain and the snow blinded him as he collided with the side of his bed.

A groaning, grinding noise made him twist around, then the shotgun report of wood breaking, splintering, and his bed's heavy headboard fell forward, as that end of his bed collapsed to the floor.

He turned wildly around now, still blinded by the sting of the glass and the snow on his face, desperate to get out of the room. "Where the hell are you?" He screamed the words. "You need to get out of here! You need to leave!"

Gone. That heaviness, that presence, gone.

The wind died; the curtains hung limp; both glass and snow sparkled across the bedroom rug. He felt blood trailing down his cheek.

He was alone.

The March wind swirled across the town park playground, scattering the laughing children. Cindy wriggled around in Martin's lap to look up at him. She gently touched one of his cheek scars. "Does it still hurt, PopPop?"

"Not any more, sweetpea. I'm all better. All healed."

"How many were there?"

"How many boo-boos?"

"No. Stit…" She struggled with the word. "How many stit-ches?"

He pointed to each one in turn. "That one was four. This one was three, and this one over here was also three. All the rest just needed boo-boo bandages."

She regarded him. "You look like a pirate."

Philippa, seated beside them, chuckled quietly. "Ready for a swing, Cindydoodle?"

"Yay!" Martin's granddaughter scrambled down off his lap, and grabbed his hand to tug on it. "Let's go, PopPop! Let's go!"

The old kiddie playground in the town park, a bit tired-looking, nothing special, but tried and true, spread out before them. "Do you miss the other playground?" he asked, as they made their way to the swings.

Cindy frowned seriously. "A little. But not that girl."

Martin stopped. "What girl?"

"The silly one, the one that made faces." She tugged at his hand. "Come *on*, PopPop!"

The face, the grin, the hundred needle teeth.

They began walking again. He surveyed the children running across the playground, all of them in color, all of them real. "There's no silly

16

girls here?" he asked.

"Course not." They reached the swings. Cindy pointed. "I wanna swing on the red one!"

Martin lifted her with a grunt, and placed her in the swing seat. "There you go," he said, taking a breath. "All set?"

"Swing me high, PopPop! Please? Swing me really high!"

He found it difficult to catch his breath, all of a sudden. He grabbed at the swing chain to keep his balance.

"Come on, PopPop! Come on!"

"Just give me a minute, sweetpea." He gripped the chain, leaning into it. "Just a minute—"

Then his daughter was there, taking him around his waist. "You okay, Dad?"

"Yeah. Just a little dizzy. A little out of breath." He shifted his weight from the chain to her. "Too soon, I guess."

"You go sit down, okay? I'll take over."

Cindy looked up over her shoulder, from one to the other. "I don't have to swing, PopPop," she said. "It's okay."

"No, you go ahead. You swing with Mommy." He gestured with his chin to the bench. "I'm just going to go sit down for a bit."

"Mommy doesn't swing me as high."

Philippa tousled her hair with her free hand. "Wanna bet?" Then to Martin, "You want me to—?"

"No. I'll be fine." He took his time, careful step after careful step, and dropped heavily to the park bench.

"There's water in the bag!" Philippa called after him.

He waved. "I'll be fine! Go swing! I'll be fine." He slumped a little, closing his eyes, and waited for the dizziness to pass.

I'll be fine, he thought. *I'm just old. I'll be fine.*

Gnat-faint, then, a whisper in his ear: "Maybe not."

Local Art

After unlocking the front door promptly at nine, Al flipped the sign hanging off it, from SORRY WE'RE CLOSED! with a frowny face, to WE'RE OPEN! with a smiley face.

The art gallery was a single storefront, located on a narrow side street, catching none of the beach traffic to the left, or the bay traffic to the right. The shaded location discouraged tourists, but Al preferred it that way. No smell of sun-block or cotton candy, no french-fry grease smudges on the bowls and vases arrayed in the window, or fingerprinted on the glass-framed watercolors displayed on the side walls and standing panels farther in. The majority of his business was with patrons who had sought out his gallery deliberately, serious customers, mostly. Those in search of art, not kitsch.

The previous owner had LOCAL ART painted in bright yellow on the outside window glass in a large, blocky font. In the right light, even though it had been scraped off, the ghost of the previous name was still visible. Perfect for the smelly, greasy, beachy crowd, actually. Al much preferred the name he had chosen to replace it – Summer Memories – painted in a respectful serif font on the front door glass only, in a less aggressive forest green.

Al returned to his desk by the jewelry case, and found his morning tea still warm. He sipped, and waited for his first customer.

He heard her before he saw her, braying in a northern accent, before the overhead bell tinkled and the front door swung open. "…What a cozy little shop! …No, not that one, a new one, easy to miss. God only knows how I found it."

A solid, short, fireplug of a woman, in a tie-dye tutu and wide-brimmed straw hat, entered the gallery. She was alone, on the phone, her back to him as she inspected the ceramics by the window. "Lunch where…? …When?" She glanced at her wristwatch. "I suppose. As long as they have gluten-free… Yeah, you too, hon. See you at eleven." She dropped her phone into her shoulder bag and began turning around, squinting. "Anybody here?"

Al rose, came around the desk, and cleared his throat. "Yes, madam."

She whirled in his direction, grabbing at her hat. "Jeez! You startled me!"

"My apologies. Welcome to Summer Memories. Were you looking for anything in particular? A painting, perhaps?"

"You perhaps right. For my condo. For over the sofa." She held her hands apart. "Something wide, you know? Maybe this big."

Al extended his hand. "We have some landscapes that size toward the rear."

She followed him. "Not too big. My sofa's a two-cushion."

Al stopped before a Westlake. A sunrise at the beach at Nags Head. "Perhaps something like this?"

She wrinkled her nose. He noticed then that she was chewing gum. She snapped it, twice. "I can look out the window and see that every day. Why would I need a painting of it?"

Al turned to an adjoining panel. "A sailboat subject, perhaps?"

"Nah. Every time I looked at that I'd get seasick." She frowned, glancing about. "You got any farm scenery? You know, barns? Cows?"

"I'm sorry, madam, no barns, no cows. We specialize in…local art."

She looked at him, chewing. "So…just beach stuff? That's it?"

"Not at all. If you will follow me?" He led her around the panel. "Perhaps a still-life. A collection of sea shells, artfully arranged? Or local wildflowers?"

The woman went over to the watercolor of wildflowers, snapping her gum. "This is nice. "Local wildflowers, you said? Too bad."

Al bent his head. "Madam?"

"Wild *weeds*, maybe, and that blue would clash with the sofa fabric." She dismissed the painting with a wave. "No thanks." She noticed the partly open door at the rear of the gallery. "You got more stuff back there?"

Al hesitated.

"Ahah!" She waved a pudgy finger at him. "The good stuff! Right?"

Al looked at her, at her face. "Let me get the light," he said, then. He did so. She smiled triumphantly as she passed him, into the rear gallery.

As she turned around to view the art on the walls, her smile vanished. "What are these? Portraits?"

"They are indeed, madam." Eleven, with room for more.

"Same artist?"

He nodded.

She waved her arms. "Why are all their eyes closed?"

He nodded again. "Why, indeed," he said, and moved closer.

Presently, he returned to the front gallery, went to the front door, locked it, and turned the sign over.

SORRY WE'RE CLOSED!

With a frowny face.

He had work to do, after all.

The Succubus

Colloquy:

    "What is it that all animals in the wild share?"

    "That's simple: hunger. They are always hungry."

Deæ Matres

Monday, October 12, 1863

The Carruthers African expedition was the frustrating and ultimately deadly disaster I feared it would be. My bout with dysentery nearly killed me, but after a fortnight of care under the supervision of Dr. Westbury at his Southampton clinic, I was finally able, under my own steam, to return to my London digs. A letter from Professor Makepiece of the New York Geographic Society awaited me there, offering a berth in his expedition to find the Gold Cities at the headwaters of the Amazon, if I could arrive at his offices by December. This gave me a fresh wind, and I quickly made passage on the first ship making a transatlantic crossing, a Star-Line freighter out of Liverpool, named Caliban.

Those few who know me well, will scarce believe that I, Arthur Spaulding, veteran of a dozen expeditions of discovery, some into the Mouth of Hell itself, would relapse on the first day of embarkation on the screw-and-sail freighter. Those first few days were a sickening blur of sweated, fouled linens, ripping headaches, delirious dreams, and, whenever I managed to get my aim true, what seemed to be a constantly full slop bucket. The cabin boy who emptied the bucket and changed my bunk linens, while I huddled in a perpetually pitching corner of my cramped cabin, always offered water and digestives. I must have drunk some, and perhaps even ate a hard biscuit or two, because by the fourth day I found myself – quite astoundingly – still alive, still in the little passenger cabin within the bowels of the Caliban, the ship cutting clean, at long last, through blessed, calm seas, ever westward for the new world, and more specifically, for the port of New York. I awoke that morning weak, but clear-headed, the fever all but gone.

A bucket of cold seawater, a hard nub of soap, and a stiff bristle brush served as my toilet, and I retrieved a fresh set of clothes from my trunk. My cabin lay below and forward of the steering house; the wardroom, if this ship followed the common plan, would be aft, just beyond the engine stack. I took the opportunity to breathe the clean ocean air by traversing the weather deck, dodging both the topside cargo and a crew who took no more notice of me than they did the breaching porpoises keeping pace with us in the ship's cresting wake. The fresh air did much to restore me, and I quickly adjusted to the steady roll of Caliban as she cut the swells as I made my way aft.

The officer's wardroom was on the main deck, one ladder down. I followed the smells of fried bacon and coffee, my awakened stomach growling in anticipation. The compartment was long and narrow, a row of portholes to starboard, with one long table and collection of chairs, and oil lamps hung above, swinging in slow arcs between hanging baskets of fruit. I found just two people at table: the sailing master, whose Christian name escaped me, but whose surname was Thorpe, and an older man, pale, with a receding hairline of limp dark hair, obviously dyed, whose name I did no know at all.

Both stood as I entered, and Thorpe indicated a chair nearest to him. His hand remained extended, and I shook it as I sat. "Mr. Spaulding is still among the living, Edward, thanks to you," he said to the other man. Then to me, "Doctor Drant, ship's surgeon mate."

"I visited you several times," Drant said, in a dour, almost sad voice. "Though in your delirium I doubt you remember."

"I am certainly glad you did, sir, and for whatever aid you provided, I am forever in your debt."

"A full breakfast's the thing." Thorpe motioned to the mess-boy holding a covered platter, who had appeared through one of the slatted doors behind him. I found myself salivating before he uncovered it, and placed fried eggs, sausages, bacon, and a slab of black pudding before me. Still, I hesitated.

"Eat!" The sailing master gestured with both hands. "We've had ours."

I fell to. Both men watched with amused expressions as I proceeded to clean my plate.

"You were in Africa, I was told," Dr. Drant said, when I took a break to drain my coffee cup.

"Yes, sir. The Carruthers expedition. We were attempting to source the Congo." I paused as the mess-boy refilled our cups.

The sailing master took the opportunity to speak up. "Did you find it?"

I shook my head as I chewed and swallowed the last of the sausage. "Just tigers, and snakes as thick as your arm. They dropped out of the trees, the nasty buggers." I put down my fork. "And graves for nearly a quarter of our party, unfortunately."

"A pity. So what, if I might ask, is your adventure in New York?"

"An offer from Professor Makepiece at the Geographic Society. He is assembling a team to find the headwaters of the Amazon."

"Ah! The mythical cities of gold."

"If we're lucky, yes. And snakes just as big, and panthers to replace the tigers."

Thorpe thumped his fist on the table as he stood. "No panthers or snakes on board Caliban, Mr. Spaulding, or chests of gold either, unfortunately. We will do our best to make your passage as uneventful as possible." He turned to the surgeon mate. "Company meeting in the Captain's mess at three bells, doctor."

"Yes sir." Drant rose, and only reseated himself after the sailing master had left the wardroom.

The door reopened almost immediately, and a short-statured man of indeterminate age entered, a passenger like myself, by his attire. His brown, straight hair was cut in a peculiar bowl shape, radiating from a small, perfectly round tonsure, much like that of a medieval monk. He nodded to the doctor, and then to me, but said nothing. The mess-boy emerged from the galley with a covered tray, which the man took from him. The mess-boy then held the door as he exited, as quickly and as silently as he had entered.

Dr. Drant saw the question in my expression. "Another passenger, Mr. Spaulding. One of only two, beside yourself. A Miss McKee is the other, a widow, I believe, and a lady of means." He gestured briefly to the door. "And her valet, of course. His name is Felix, I was told. American, both of them, like yourself."

"A lady of means?"

Drant nodded. "She's taken all four of the forward cabins. For privacy, I suppose."

"Leaving two empty?"

Drant nodded again. "And she is striking, I must say; I only had a glimpse. A true beauty."

"Then I shall look forward to meeting her."

"I doubt you will. She takes her meals in her cabin, as you just saw. I only glimpsed her when she and this Felix fellow embarked, and I've yet to see her topside since, to take the air."

I leaned back to let the mess-boy clear my place, and refill my coffee cup. "A mystery, then. Interesting."

"Not as interesting as the cargo she's shipping back. If you've been topside yourself you've no doubt seen it."

"What would I have been looking for?"

"Her cargo is lashed to the weather deck just aft of the stack, hidden under the canvas tarpaulins." He pointed up. "Just above us, as a matter of fact."

"I noticed them, certainly, but I just assumed—"

"Stones. Huge things. Actual Druid stones. Three of them. I watched when they were craned aboard. Mr. Gosforth, the cargo master, referred to them as The Three Sisters."

"Druid stones? Prehistoric, you mean. Some call them dolmens, I've heard."

"I'm sure they have many names. I'm also sure a Cornish farmer must have had a good laugh, taking her silver."

"What could she possibly want with such things?"

"I have no idea."

I took a swallow of coffee. "What else are we carrying?"

"You would have to ask Mr. Gosforth. On previous voyages it was whiskey and wool." Dr. Drant wiped his mouth, tossed his napkin to the table, and stood with a rueful smile. "And textiles." He favored me with a dramatic wink. "Dyed blue."

"Better than gray, sir."

Drant laughed. "You Americans. A civil war bloodier than ours ever was. And tigers, snakes, and standing stones!"

He left me, then, to finish my coffee. I did so, but not before glancing up…

Throughout the next week, every morning if the weather permitted, I took my exercise, gathering strength, strolling the weather deck of Caliban. I encountered no beautiful stranger at the rails, however, nor her monk-tonsured valet, but more than once I stopped and laid a hand on the salt-crusted canvas covering the Druid stones. What odd cargo! And for what purpose?

On the Thursday of that week I discovered a small aft deck, no more than a railed section of roof, actually, sprouting two stovepipe stacks nearly chest-high, and smelling pleasantly of woodsmoke and roasting meat. I surmised that this deck, this roof, tucked behind the main weather deck and about a yard higher, must cover the galley. Because it was out of the way of all the deck crew activities, and nearly flat, I decided to call it mine, my deck, my personal domain. I brought up a small folding chair from the wardroom, prepared to spend many a daylight hour undisturbed, watching the sky and the sea, looking expectantly for land, or even a land bird, though I knew both were still far to the west, and days off.

The following morning I found my chair out of its storage place under the lip of the weather deck. It was unfolded, brazenly placed out on the deck. I also smelled of…perfume? Something faint, but heady enough to pierce the smells of the luncheon preparations from the stacks. Was I now sharing my private domain with my mysterious fellow passenger, perhaps?

After dinner that evening, after watching Felix, the valet, return the mysterious Miss McKee's cloth-covered tray, and after refusing the offer of one of the bos'n mate's foul-smelling cheroots, I went outside, into the cold night breeze, and made my way aft.

The crescent moon was low in the east, anchoring the great blade of stars that cleaved the heavens. As I approached my private deck a scent caught in my nostrils, the same perfume as the one I had smelled before, lingering on the folding chair, before being ripped away on the wind. I smiled in the darkness, coming at last to the low railing above the short row of galley portholes.

And I saw her above me, leaning against the railing, a silhouette against the stars. Her long hair was loose about her in a wild tangle, and the scant light afforded by the meager sliver of moon wasn't enough to reveal her features. I could nevertheless discern that her attention was directed not down to me, but out, to the far southern horizon. I might as well have been a bollard, bolted to the deck below her.

I raised my voice into the wind. "Excuse me. May I come up?"

She looked down to me at last, and all I could see of her features was the moonlight reflected in her eyes. "No, sir." Her voice was surprisingly contralto. "You may not."

I felt a hand on my arm, and I confess I sprang away, but it was only the valet. "Madam prefers her privacy," he said.

From above: "Don't hurt him, Felix."

The valet extended a hand toward the bow.

I turned to the woman above, and bowed stiffly. "Pardon me." I left them, and as I strode along the deck I had an urge to look back–an urge quite unlike me–but of course I did not.

On the fifth day of that week, during one of my deck walks, Mr. Thorpe motioned to me from the quarterdeck just aft of the wheelhouse. He had a long black telescope in hand. "You should see this," he called down to me. "They rarely get so close!"

I ascended the nearest ladder to join him, took the offered scope, and trained it on the spot of ocean where he pointed. At first, all I could see were waves crested with foam, but then a dark shape broke the surface, jetting a tall plume of white breath. The wind was in my mouth, but I shouted through it: "What kind of beast is it?"

"Sperm! A pod of them. I've counted four so far."

"Amazing, sir." I returned the scope to him. "We are so alone out here in the middle of the sea, the whales must be a welcome sight."

He nodded. "They're lucky we're not hunting them."

I gestured to the western horizon. "We're lucky we're not being hunted ourselves."

"What do you mean?"

"Surely we are approaching American waters by now."

"Ah! Your insurrectionist war." Thorpe's tone grew serious. "England is officially neutral, of course. Both parties can plainly see we fly Her Majesty's colors."

"But you are also playing both sides of the board, are you not? You sell arms to both sides, buy cotton from the South, and beaver pelts from the North. Neither party can be happy with such a situation. Particularly the Confederacy."

The sailing master clapped his free hand on my shoulder. "We've done this passage crossing many times, Mr. Spaulding. The Union has never given us cause to be concerned."

"But the South? The rebels?"

"For anyone who confronts us we have cannon and shot, and sharp blades." His grip tightened briefly on my shoulder. "No need to be concerned."

Alas…

I was startled from a dreamless sleep by the insistent clamoring of the ship's bell, and the pounding run of crewmen along the passageway, and across the deck above me. The bell was replaced by a klaxon horn, three blasts in quick succession. I swung out of my bed, rubbing the sleep from my face. What was the emergency? Good God, we had a hundred fathoms at least of cold Atlantic beneath our keel, and were still several days from landfall and safe harbor. Could it be fire, or an iceberg wandering too far south?

I dressed hurriedly in the darkness, my breath clouding before me as I struggled with my boots, extra sweater, and oilskin coat. Not an iceberg, surely; it was barely Autumn, and we hadn't tracked that far north, had we? But a fire… One of the deck mates saw me step out into the passageway, and gave me a savage wave. "Back in your cabin, sir! There's no safe place for you on deck!"

"But what's the emergency?"

"No business of yours. Back into your cabin!"

I followed his order, if grudgingly, having to be content to sit on my bed and listen only to the bedlam unfolding around me. By interpreting mates' and officers' orders, some through megaphones, others just yelled, it was soon clear that a hostile ship had been sighted, and had made an aggressive course change to intercept Caliban. African pirates took no prisoners. Dear God–!

Below me, cannons were rolling into position, their chocks pounded in place. Extra canvas was being unfurled, and no doubt more coal was being shoveled into the boiler furnaces. Caliban was both a sail- and screw-powered vessel, and a freighter by design, not a warship; speed to outrun, to escape, not cannon-fire to fight, was what was needed most.

I finally opened my cabin door, and found the passageway empty. I made my way aft, staying belowdecks, and only emerged into the open air of the weather deck when I was nearly at the stern. My private deck was my destination, and I climbed the ladder to it blindly in the softening dark.

I immediately went to the port side, where I could see the violet bruise of an eventual dawn creeping along the eastern horizon. Silhouetted there, I just made out a ship, in full sail, on a tangent course to our own. The lookouts, with their well-trained eyes, and those with telescopes in the wheelhouse, had already identified it, hence the alarm bells and klaxon, and the crew was assembled at the ready. A pirate ship or Confederate frigate, it was yet too far for me to tell.

"A hand, please."

I spun around to see a figure at the deck railing behind me, a feminine hand reaching out of the darkness. I recrossed the deck in three strides, and took it. In moments, in a flurry of sweet-scented satin and petticoats, Miss McKee stood on the gently rolling deck before me. Her valet clambered over the railing after her, and made to stand between us, but she held him back with just a touch to his shoulder. It was too dark for me to see her face clearly, but a mass of darker curls framed it, and the violet smudge of the pre-dawn reflected off her eyes. "Mr. Spaulding," she said, with a hint of a smile in her voice. "We meet again. I am Miss McKee."

"You should have stayed below, madam," I said. "It's not safe for you here."

"On the contrary, sir." She gestured out to the approaching ship. "Here is exactly where I should be." She moved across to the port side, her full attention on the ship. "That is the Confederate Sailing Ship Chattanauga." She turned to address me as I gained her side. "A cruiser of twenty guns."

"It's still too far for me to make any detail. How can you–?"

"They've been stalking us these past two days."

"Again, madam, how can you know this? Clearly this is the first time it's been observed."

"And being seen at last makes all the difference, sir. Being seen is their most dire mistake."

She was speaking in riddles. I decided not to humor her. "Before the first shot is made, I insist you and your man go below."

Miss McKee smiled again. "Theirs or ours?"

"It makes no difference. A lucky ball—"

She put a finger to my lips. Her hand, when I had grasped it before, had been unnaturally cold, and her finger, now, was even more so. She turned from me again, her attention on the Confederate cruiser.

Behind me, her valet cleared his throat. "Perhaps you should step back, sir." He spoke so quietly the wind fairly whipped his words away. I was about to give an appropriate riposte, when I saw, in the distance, a tremendous, momentary blue-white light limn the Confederate ship, waves and clouds like a photographer's sodium flash. It half-blinded me with its brilliance, so much so I had to look away. Something on the Confederate ship had gone horribly wrong. The flash was followed in moments by the air-rending crack and thunder of the explosion, hardly gentled by its travel. Three more explosions followed in succession. I once again had to look away, but Miss McKee, illuminated by the glare, looked calmly out to the carnage unfolding before us, at the rim of the night.

Seeing her face and features at last, I found myself staggered by her ungodly beauty. Like a thunderclap itself, I was instantly lost. It was only with the greatest effort, with my cheeks burning, that I could turn my attention from her to the scene before us. Through roiling smoke, the still distant fires from the blasts showed what was left of the Confederate cruiser: it was broken in two pieces, both sinking quickly, in a vast area of flaming debris. Another flash, another thunderous explosion, and the larger of the pieces was gone.

"Surely," I began, turning once more to Miss McKee, but I stopped myself, my mouth agape. The light from the distant fires, and the burgeoning dawn, washed over her, but there was something more, some other *glow*, emanating from her. Her eyes were wide, her smile now a broad, toothy grin, her arms outstretched, as though embracing the horrific scene before her and gathering it in. *She's eating*, was my only thought. *She's eating…this.*

My backward steps encountered the valet, and he took hold of me to keep us both from falling over the low rail. This brought me back into the world, and I was aware of the shouts from the crew of Caliban, calls for lifeboat crews, fire teams, as the ship began a turn to starboard, not on a course to flee, now, but to intercept, to rescue anyone who might have survived.

Miss McKee turned from the rail at last, silhouetted, now, her macabre grin gone, her face in blue shadow. "There are none," she said.

"Madam—"

"Survivors, Mr. Spaulding. They wanted our blood, our death, but instead have been served a meal of their own. No survivors. All gone. All dead."

The smoke from the still floating, flaming remains of the destroyed ship was reaching us at last, carried on a swift wind. Miss McKee staggered, then, but her valet was at her side, putting his arm around her. She leaned into him, just as a voice – some sailor or mate – yelled up from the weather deck, "What in holy hell are you ragbags doing up there?"

"Let me—"

"No, sir." Mr. Felix's voice was as hard and cold as the wind. "You will not touch her. No one shall."

The next morning, breaking my fast earlier than usual, I found the wardroom nearly full. Every master and mate not on duty was there. All of them, including Mr. Thorpe, the sailing master, were subdued, speaking to others near them only in monosyllables or grunts, or not at all. I had questions aplenty, but I knew this was not the time or place for them.

I don't remember eating, or making my way forward, but I found myself in the forward passageway, outside the four cabin doors, all of them closed.

I knocked on the nearest one, three times, but received no reply. I turned to the cabin opposite, but my knocking there also drew no response. I hesitated. What would I say if a door opened? What would I do?

I went to the next door, and knocked as before. This time I heard movement from within, and a turn of a lock. The door opened mere inches, revealing part of a face: a watery blue eye, wiry hair like a bird's nest atop a high forehead, and an impossibly thin mustache. A stranger, a third passenger I had not known about. "I—" I began, hesitating.

Behind me, then, a voice intruded. "Sir." I turned, and as I did so I heard the door behind me close. The master's mate stood at the near end of the passageway, one hand resting on the grip of his holstered pistol. "This passage is closed," he said.

I looked from him to the door, then back again. "I don't understand."

"It is private. No one is allowed entry. Captain's express orders, sir."

The look in the master's mate's eyes, and the tone of his voice, spoke volumes. I had been about to knock on the door a second time, but I lowered my fist. "My apologies, sir.."

The master's mate stepped aside. "This way."

He followed me back to my cabin.

Wednesday, December 9, 1863

Professor Makepiece offered me a cigar, which I refused with a polite wave. "You appear preoccupied, Arthur," he said, as he waved the waiter over to indicate our nearly empty glasses.

"There was a woman on board the freighter. I can't get her out of my thoughts."

"An affair of the heart during the crossing. You?"

I waved my hand again. "Not that. We hardly spoke, and only met twice. No. It was the cargo she was transporting from England."

"Of what sort? Antiques? Objets d'art?"

"Stones. Large dolmens. Twenty feet in length at least. Three of them."

"Ahh." The professor lit his cigar, nodding as he did so. "Deæ Matres," he said then, extinguishing his match. "Early Rome. Third century BC, I believe. The Maiden, the Mother, and the Crone."

"These were natural stones, not statues; no carving on them whatsoever, just the weathering of centuries. I watched the unloading."

"The Romans stole from everyone, particularly the peoples they conquered. The Celts called them The Three Sisters. Something about the phases of the Moon: wax–full–wane." Makepiece pondered the end of his cigar for a moment. "Someone mentioned the transportation of large stones the other day, as a matter of fact." He looked past me, and I had the manners not to turn. "Edwards! Can we bother you for a moment? There's a good man."

A rather rotund gentleman approached our table, sizing me up with a single look. We had met before, apparently, but I could not place him. "I have guests, Peter," he began.

"Just a question, just a moment. There's the good fellow. Last week, we shared that table with Tennier. You recall, certainly. He mentioned someone on the Island requiring the installation of some rather cumbersome stones."

"Yes. Three stones, I believe. Huge things, interesting mechanical challenge."

"Indeed. Can you remember, did he mention where?"

"In Kings, not too far from the city cemeteries they're laying out. A property in Bushwick, I believe he said."

I spoke up. "Bushwick the village, at the edge of Brooklyn?"

Edwards nodded. "Off one of those damn Roman-straight avenues they are surveying everywhere."

Professor Makepiece beamed at me through his cigar smoke. "Surely that can't be a coincidence? Surely that is where your stones have found a home?"

It had snowed throughout the night, and only trailed off to a murky, steel-grey morning during my breakfast in the hotel's dining room.

"I expect you will be staying in today, sir," the waiter said, refilling my coffee cup.

No. It had to be today. Professor Makepiece's instructions on the expedition's departure for South America were clear and steadfast. In three days I would be on my way to the southern continent, and the vast jungled Amazon basin, and, hopefully, a share in a fortune in gold and treasure.

The door captain secured a two-seat hansom whose driver agreed to the fare only because I required a one-way journey to the East River docks. Because of the snow, a trip of ten minutes took three times as long, but the driver got me to a ferry that was still loading for its trip across. Like everyone else aboard, I huddled in the lounge by the cabin stoves until we were secured to the ferry's Red Hook slip. From there, with no hansoms in evidence, I walked.

The County of Kings I traversed pretended to be a brother to the proper city across the river, but was in reality just a ragged collection of villages and small farms crossed with wide, incongruous paved avenues. The main routes were more or less clear, and I soon found the one named Bushwick, after the hamlet it sprang from. It went south to a raw rail track still under construction. To the left was a side street, equally raw. Along its western side were a series of large, sprawling homes of modern design, all of them on large acre-or-more plots, and all of them facing a wide, rolling succession of potter's fields and cemeteries beyond the rail line, but with no accompanying church I could see. Closest to the tracks, the headstones of the proper graves large enough to reach daylight, were capped with thick hats of white. I wondered who would be buried there, in what appeared to be unconsecrated ground.

A four-horse wagon laden with barrels of what, by the smell, could only have been beer, passed me, and I almost jumped on its panel for a ride, but then I saw them, amid a stand of young sycamores. The stones, the dolmens, the Deæ Matres. They wore their own snow caps beyond a large, newly-built house, crowning what could only be described in the flat landscape as a man-made hill, a mound. The property, at least three acres of young trees and brush, was enclosed by a high, wrought-iron fence. I trudged along it until I was as close to the stones as possible without trespassing. They stood tall and straight, braving this New World snowstorm as stoically as they must have done the English ones, through the centuries, in the Old.

Seeing no lights or other signs of life in the house, and no one visible on the avenue, I made the rash decision to climb the fence. In moments, careful of my grip on the cold, wet iron, I was safely over. I approached the stones, and went among them. The snow around us was just drifting veils, the wind a quiet moan. I touched one of them, ran my fingers down its rough and pitted surface. As I did so I realized they were spaced too far apart for me to reach another. Even so, I also realized the spacing of the stones, their placement in the ground, was not regular. I imagined the mysterious Miss McKee, pointing to the ground, directing the workers. "Here," she said, "exactly here."

I ran my coat cuffs down to cover my hands, placed them akimbo, and looked up at the stones. "Why," I asked aloud, to no-one but myself, my voice lost in the stinging, windblown snow.

"An answer comes with a price, Mr. Spaulding."

I whirled around, and saw her a few yards away, standing taller than I remembered her. The falling snow fairly hid her face, her features, her eyes. I could not meet her gaze, could not look into her eyes. I simply couldn't.

She approached, more a wraith than a woman, then paused, still yards away. "You can still leave," she said. "If you want."

I didn't move.

Her laughter was low, and endless.

My last thought, as she again walked toward me, her face clearing at last, as her eyes grew to envelope me, to envelope everything, my last living thought was: *she's hungry*.

The Rest Is Yours

Wednesday, June 8, 1864; Augusta County, Virginia

"Open the window, Artur," she said to Mr. Felix. "It's become stifling."

"There will be flies, ma'am."

"I can deal with flies." She gave her fan a final, futile wave. "But not this heat."

He snapped the latch, and the glass rattled down. The carriage immediately filled with the stench of fresh manure and horse piss. She pulled a kerchief from her sleeve to cover her nose and mouth.

"The horses—" Mr. Felix began.

"Picked a most inopportune moment." She waved the kerchief to the window as the carriage bumped over a rough patch of roadway. "Leave it open. It will pass."

The Valley Turnpike thereafter went mostly straight and sometimes level, with clear views to the east of patchwork fields, and the rumpled blue mountains beyond. She watched, expressionless, as their passage caused a murder of crows to rise in flapping, squawking confusion from a field of young corn. "You'd hardly know there was a war on," she said.

Mr. Felix pointed south. "I can see smoke ahead."

She struck the roof of the carriage with her parasol's handle. The carriage slowed, and the hatch opened on a square of blinding sky. The voice of the driver was rough, but high. "Yes, miss?"

"How close are we?"

"To the battlefield? Two mile. Just east of that rise, there, ahead of us. You can see the smoke."

"What about Piedmont?"

"Piedmont, miss?"

"The town. We were told it was the Battle of Piedmont. We were hoping to secure lodging there."

The carriage came to a squeaking halt, and the hatch framed the driver's face. "Pardon me for saying, but that makes no sense, miss."

"What do you mean?"

"Piedmont's no town. It's just a crossroad. Port Republic, now, that's a town of sorts. And Staunton, eight mile or so south, that's a right and proper town. Railroad, and two hotels, take your pick."

"Who holds it?"

"Union, miss, last I heard."

She looked to Mr. Felix, who shrugged. She said, "Take us to the battlefield first, then. And Staunton, after."

"Like I said, miss, Staunton's eight mile—"

Her eyes flashed. "Is there a question? A problem?"

"No, miss." The driver's face disappeared from the hatch. "As you wish, miss." The hatch came down with a soft thud, and the carriage began rolling once more.

Their early morning journey down the turnpike from the train junction at Harrisonburg had been largely uneventful. Their only encounter of note had been with a squad of bluecoats, led by a middle-aged Lieutenant, his belly straining against his sweat-stained uniform blouse, tobacco juice dribbled and dried in his beard. Brigadier General Sullivan's letter of passage she had produced for him to puzzle over had turned out to be enough, as she knew it would be. Handing it back to her through the carriage window and doffing his hat, he had returned to his men, bivouacked in the shade of the trees. He said something to them that elicited scattered laughter as they passed. She stiffened. Mr. Felix flashed her a warning look, but it was too late; she was already feeding. The silent shrieks of the soldiers died, eventually, like them, with distance.

Their journey moved from the turnpike to a rougher, more narrow track. "It's the Eastern Road, miss," their driver explained, during a pause to let the horses drink from a shaded creek. "Take you to Port Republic, it does."

She was forced to show the letter of passage two more times before their carriage was allowed to finally reach the scene of the recent battle. The sky was a hard, hot blue, the wind nonexistent, the air heavy with the stench of fire smoke and the already rotting dead. Beyond, jagged triangles of log and rail fences marked the field verge. A sea of bloated corpses, both whole and in pieces, human and equine, were strewn across a random pattern of artillery craters. Wooded hills rose on either side of the fields; broken cannon poked out of the tree shade on the western side. A farmhouse, barn and collection of outbuildings lay along the far southern edge of the nearest field. The majority of Union troops were gathered there, under summer tents, and around several large, burning campfires.

She banged her parasol handle on the carriage roof, and the carriage rolled to a halt. The hatch squeaked open. "Miss?"

"Here will do."

"Yes, miss." The hatch shut, and they heard the driver climb down. He opened the carriage door on her side. "Ground's dry enough," he said.

She pointed with her parasol. "I only see soldiers. No citizenry but us?"

"This was a Union victory on Virginia soil. The smart ones have no business here." He saw her expression. "No disrespect intended, miss."

She ignored his outstretched hand, and clambered to the ground. Mr. Felix followed. The driver and he stared at one another briefly, then Mr. Felix pulled his purse from his jacket, and counted several Union-minted silver dollars into the driver's glove. "Half now, as we agreed."

"I'll be taking my team back to the stream we passed over earlier."

She opened her parasol. "We won't be long. Give us an hour."

The driver doffed his hat, then remounted his carriage. It produced a considerable cloud of dust, turning awkwardly, momentarily engulfing them as they stood in the tall grass beside the track. She looked to Mr. Felix, and gave her head a single shake. *We still need him.*

They watched two hay wagons being loaded with the Union dead by soldiers wearing long leather aprons. Beyond them, a crew of prisoners, some in uniform, some not, were digging a long trench under the direction of a half-dozen Union soldiers on horseback.

"Under this sun," Mr. Felix said, waving at the flies.

She took her kerchief out, and covered her nose and mouth.

One of the hay wagons creaked toward them, pulled by two immense dray horses. The bodies and body parts were piled high. The driver, with two chevrons on his sleeve, spat a long stream of tobacco juice into the grass, close to where they stood. As he grinned through gapped teeth she locked eyes with him. His grin faltered, then became a grimace, and a sudden guttural moan escaped his throat. He appeared to crumple, to shrink.

Mr. Felix laid a hand on her arm, and she covered it with her own. The driver slumped back, into the pile of bodies. The dray horses slowed, and stopped.

A soldier on horseback, an officer by his braid, approached the wagon. He called to a group of enlisted soldiers tending a nearby fire. One of them trotted over, climbed up to the wagon seat, and took the reins the first driver had dropped, and began, slowly, to turn the horses.

While there was still time, she closed her eyes and fed on the remains of the dead in the wagon bed as it passed. Mr. Felix held her arm, steadying her. When she opened her eyes again the mounted officer was just yards away. "Are you unwell, miss?"

"On the contrary, sir." She tilted her parasol back, and shaded her eyes to look up at him. "I am extraordinarily fine. You are kind to ask."

"The air isn't the sweetest," he said. "It's taking a toll on us all."

"I am perfectly well, truly. Thank you for your concern."

The officer leaned and extended a gloved hand. "First Lieutenant Clarence Maxwell, 20th Pennsylvania."

She looked at the hand, then extended her own, and they touched gloved fingers. "Iona McKee."

The officer's saddle creaked as he straightened. "It's best to stand clear, Miss McKee." He nodded toward the trees behind her. "I recommend the shade beyond."

"We came a long way to see this, sir."

"How far have you come?"

"New York. Brooklyn. We're citizens, sir. Patriots, not rebels."

Lieutenant Maxwell regarded them both. Then he turned to the men by the fire, and pointed to the tallest among them. "Private!"

The soldier exchanged looks with the others around him, then approached, and saluted. "Sir?"

"Your name?"

"Smythe, sir. Edward Smythe."

"Accompany our guests, Private Smythe. See that they stay clear of harm's way."

"Sir." The private saluted again, and the officer nodded to her, then wheeled his horse around, and left them. "I can't take you onto the battlefield proper," the soldier said to Mr. Felix. "It's not safe."

"Please speak to the lady, sir," Mr. Felix said.

Turning to her, the Private Smythe cast his eyes down. "Unexploded ordnance, ma'am. Star shells and such." He hesitated. "And we're still recovering the bodies."

"I understand, Private Smythe. Perhaps we can walk along the verge and you can tell us of your experience in the battle."

"There's not much to tell, but I'll do my best, ma'am."

They began walking.

"What regiment are you with, Private Smythe?"

"28th Ohio, ma'am. Large bore artillery. We engaged on the second day."

"I've visited Ohio. Cleveland."

The private looked surprised, even pleased. "I'm from Strongsville, just south of there."

"Wonderful country. The lake…" She swept her parasol to include the blue mountains to the east. "The beauty of it rivals even this."

"You're very kind, ma'am."

"But you were about to describe your experience in battle."

"It was as I said, ma'am. There's not much to see from a gun-loader's position. Discharges, smoke, the yelling, men screaming, horses too, more discharges when we got the elevation right." He wiped at his mustache. "Even with the greased cotton stuffed in, my ears are still ringing."

She paused to look at him. "You poor man."

He bowed his head briefly.

She pointed across to the farm. "I'm curious about the yellow flags, the ones by the barn."

"They're using the cow barn for the field hospital, ma'am."

"At Gettysburg the field hospital flags were red, weren't they, Artur?"

"I believe so," Mr. Felix said.

Smythe shrugged. "I wouldn't know, sir."

They resumed walking.

"Who is caring for the enemy's dead?" she asked, after a moment.

"The crows, ma'am, pardon my plain speaking." Smythe gestured across the field to the prisoners digging the long ditch. "They'll end up there, is my guess."

"A mass grave."

"A better end than they deserve. Traitors, ma'am. Traitors to our great nation."

"Indeed." She smiled at him. "Can you give us a moment, Private Smythe?"

"Of course, ma'am." Smythe stepped away.

She waved her fan at the orbiting midges. In a quiet voice, she said, "I'm afraid we're too late, Artur."

"I feared so. This is no Agincourt."

"No." She took in a breath through her nose, behind her fan, and let it out slowly. "Still. Perhaps you can keep our poor Private Smythe back? Give me room?"

"Of course." Mr. Felix turned, and gestured to the soldier to follow into the shadow of the trees. "She wants to be alone with her prayers," he said, and Smythe nodded his understanding.

She turned to the field, lowering, then closing her parasol. She knew more than a few eyes were on her, on this splash of white and pale blue satin standing just beyond the carnage. For this reason, she chose not to raise her arms.

The cloud of midges, and then the flies, began dropping from the air, dying all around her. She closed her eyes, filled her lungs, and slowly clenched her fists.

And fed.

By this time, two days after the battle, most of the dead had fled beyond her grasp, lost to the shadow lands, or worse. But enough of them remained behind, lost and wandering, she could still feast upon...upon their sadness, and anger, and aching grief...but most sweetly of all, their utter *terror*. Like an unseen, unfelt breeze, her hunger swept the battlefield before her, and the one beyond. Near the farmhouse a horse screamed and bolted, nearly throwing its rider. The cows lowed in a ragged chorus. Crows picking among the bodies were alarmed into sudden flight, where they pinwheeled, and fell.

Was it just a minute, or five, or even ten? She wasn't sure, but she knew when she was finally full…

Too full, perhaps. She raised her hand to cover an appropriate scream, and collapsed into the grass. In a moment she heard the sound of running, through slitted eyes saw mud-smeared boots gathering around her, then Mr. Felix's voice above the murmurings of concern: "She needs air, gentlemen. Please! Give her air."

"Perhaps away, sir." That was Private Smythe. "Back to the trees. The air is cooler under the trees."

She felt hands lifting her, helping her sit upright. She let her eyes flutter open. "Oh dear! Did I faint? Oh dear!"

"Can you stand, ma'am?"

"In a moment, I think…in a moment."

Mr. Felix had recovered her parasol, and he held it over her. They exchanged a look. He straightened, motioning to Smythe. "Our driver is back along the East Road, watering his horses at a stream."

"I know the place, sir. It's not far."

"Can you please go fetch him? I think Miss McKee has had enough for today."

She almost laughed at that. Enough, indeed! Instead, she smiled at the private, a smile that radiated, penetrated, captured. A gift. "If you would, please, Private Smythe," she said, in a silken voice meant for his ears alone. "I will be forever in your debt."

"Yes, ma'am…" His face flushed, and his mouth hung open for just a moment. Then he stumbled, turning. "Whatever you wish, ma'am."

She leaned close to Mr. Felix, and whispered in his ear, "Are you hungry, Artur?"

He nodded, his mouth a thin, bloodless line.

"Get me settled, there in the shade." She waved her hand like shooing a fly. "The rest is yours."

"Yes, ma'am," Mr. Felix said. "Thank you, ma'am."

Behind Me

Coming home from university, home, such a transient word, since in the Spring mother moved from the home where I was born to a new house, abandoning mine and my late father's memories for something new, something expensive, sprawling and flashy by the river walk. 'New', more transience, since this pile of brick and marble and carved stone was in fact very very *old*. Old with baggage.

Old like her. And also like her, not truly a home.

The first time I heard the voice, I was walking one of my increasingly frequent last miles to confront my mother's wrath. Some nonsense about spending her heard-won wealth at university studies I clearly didn't appreciate, and would certainly never use to best advantage. The usual.

I had gotten off the bus (yes, my mother's allowance did not include having my own car) at 3rd and Adams, and was waiting for the light, when a voice said behind me said, "Watch out, silly boy."

Irritated, I turned to see who had spoken. A businessman stood there, looking at his phone with a preoccupied expression. "Excuse me?" I said to him.

He looked up. "Pardon?"

"Did you just tell me to watch out?"

The light changed, and without replying the businessman brushed by me and crossed the street.

How rude! I watched him go down Adams and lose himself in the crowd. How very rude indeed! Silly boy? I stopped for another light at 6th. This time there was no one behind me when the same voice said, "I could push you." It was a casual statement, with no emotion behind it, no malice. Although I knew no one was there, I turned around, "Where are you?"

Silence.

"*Who* are you?"

I heard a quiet chuckle. "It's green, silly boy."

And so it was. Half-expecting a playful push between my shoulder blades that didn't come, I crossed the street, silly boy that I apparently was, toward my mother's home.

I next heard my invisible companion during dinner. 'High table', my mother called it, with a note in her voice to remind me how fortunate I was to be there, to dine with her.

Oliver had just poured the wine and retreated to the kitchen when she began her attack. "I spoke with the Dean the other day."

Ah. Here it comes. No secrets between us, apparently. "How is the old bird?"

"Concerned with your effort, or should I say the lack of." She put down her glass. "Should I be concerned?"

"She doesn't like you very much," the voice behind me whispered.

Not at all, actually. Not, at, all.

"Absolutely not, Mother," I said, with a winning smile.

Her expression could have cut crystal. "If you expect me to continue remunerating the University to fund your spotty attendance..."

"Quite the bitch, isn't she."

Yes. Oh yes.

"I promise, Mother," I said. "I will apply myself."

Oliver arrived with the soup. He moved like a ghost, making no sound at all.

Two spoons remained beside my bowl. I chose with care.

It was a chicken consume, and Oliver had made a decent job of it.

"Sip the soup, Gerald," my mother said, in quiet irritation. "The spoon must never pass the lips."

The voice whispered in my ear, "The spoon would do it."

I wanted to ask him (for it was, now, clearly a 'he') for what, exactly, the spoon would do, but he seemed to anticipate my silent question.

"Her eye, silly boy. Scoop it right out, into her soup!"

I considered it.

"Your soup," my mother said.

"Yes, Mother?"

"It's getting cold."

Silence, now, behind me.

"Yes, Mother," I said.

After the main course, the uneasy silence remained, hanging in the air between us. I played with my dessert spoon. Mother frowned. Finally, she said, "Go see what is taking Oliver so long."

"Yes, Mother," said the voice behind me.

"Whatever you say, Mother," I said.

The rear hall, lined with a variety of antique mirrors, led to the kitchen. I found Oliver at the sink, with steam rising around him.

"Getting a head start on cleanup are we, Oliver old man?"

"Idle hands, sir," Oliver said over his shoulder, banging pans. "The soufflé is almost done."

What I required was easily found.

"Mother sent me to ask how long." His back was still to me. I saw a thin stain of perspiration down the spine of his otherwise spotless shirt. "So easy," the voice behind me whispered. "So easy." Indeed, I thought. But not yet. After, perhaps.

Oliver glanced at the clock on the wall. "Two minutes, sir. Three at most."

"Excellent," the voice behind me said. "Plenty of time."

"Soufflés have a life of their own," I said. "Or so I've been told."

"Indeed they do, sir," Oliver said, reaching for a towel as he turned. But I had already left the kitchen.

The double-mirror reflections in the hall mirrors let me see what was behind me, at last.

Not a 'he', but an 'it'.

Something long and shiny. Something sharp.

But who could be holding it?

Why, *me*, of course. Silly boy.
Only me.

Addenda

Story Notes

Maybe Not
There is a public park in Rockingham, Virginia, east of Harrisonburg, just off Route 33, located in a parcel of land that that was once a family farm. They recently added a playground there, right next to an old, abandoned family graveyard, fenced off to keep the kiddies out. Next to, I wondered, watching my grandsons play, or on top of?

Local Art
Vacationing with family in Nags Head, North Carolina, we would sometimes drive past this small art gallery on a side street just a block from the ocean beach. It had a cheaply-made window sign that read, in Day-Glo green: LOCAL ART.

The Succubus Stories
Both of these historical stories were part of an aborted horror/super-natural novel I was writing during COVID, called "3 Stones". The stories were meant to introduce characters who would play major roles in the modern setting of the novel itself. The novel will probably never

be finished, but at least these stories, complete in themselves, remain.

Behind Me
I woke very early one recent morning with the last four sentences of this story repeating in my head. It was clearly the end of a story, I decided, rolling out of bed to write them down. But why? And how should it begin?

Colophon

This book was designed and laid out on an M-1-Max Mac-Studio, using Affinity Designer 2 and Publisher 2 software, V.2.5.7.

The font family used for the text is Baskerville, and the font family used for the headlines is Gill Sans.

The illustration on unnumbered page 6 was drawn by the author with pencil on bristol board, in 2011.

Bio

Keith Minnion sold his first story to Asimov's in 1979. His most recent story collection is Under The Wing & Others, published in 2022. His third novel, Ameri-Scares Pennsylvania: The Ghost Notes, was published in 2024. Keith is a former magazine and book illustrator, DoD Project Manager, GPO Senior Print Contract Specialist, and officer in the U.S. Navy. He currently lives in Virginia, pursuing woodworking, painting, writing, and creating video content for two YouTube channels (that only a select few people subscribe to!).

https://www.keithminnionstudio.com/books
youtube.com/@keithminnionwoodshop
youtube.com/@keithminnionstudioart

Made in the USA
Middletown, DE
20 December 2024